The. Magic Boot

Written by Rémy Simard
Illustrated by Pierre Pratt

Annick Press
Toronto • New York

In a little country where people were very poor, there lived a woman who was terribly discouraged. Her son Pipo had enormous feet—and they would not stop growing.

Pipo's feet grew so fast that he could win a race without even moving.

When Maria, Pipo's little sister, went off to work in the fields, the boy and his mother would go begging for money to buy shoes.

"Money for his poor feet, money for his poor feet!" called his mother to the people walking by.

A good fairy who happened to be in the neighbourhood decided to help the boy, whose feet by now were as long as water skis.

From his window next door Roberto, green with envy, watched as the good fairy with two waves of her magic wand made two magnificent red boots appear. He couldn't believe his eyes, his ears, or his nose!

"Here, Pipo, here's a pair of magic boots," said the fairy. "When they get too small, just water them and they will grow. But be careful. Don't water them too much..."

ipo was so happy that he went skipping off in his new boots. "I wish I had boots like that, too," grumbled jealous Roberto, who had been spying on Pipo.

ithout thinking of the fairy's warning, Pipo jumped in all the puddles. Splish! Splash! Splush! But as the water licked his boots...

...they grew bigger and bigger and became much too large for Pipo's feet. At the last puddle, he tripped and fell—and came face to face with a bunch of enormous, hairy toes.

"**A**h ha! Finally, my dinner has arrived!" roared the terrible, horrible owner of the toes.

"Oh, please, Mr. Ogre, don't eat me. I'm skinny and bony and really dirty."

But Hector the Ogre loved to eat skinny, bony, dirty children, even if the dirt did get stuck between his teeth.

He thought Pipo would make an excellent meal.

"ait a minute, Mr. Ogre, I have a bargain for you," said Pipo, who was quite a little businessman. "I'll give you my boots if you don't eat me."

"I don't need boots!" the ogre roared.

"An ogre without boots is no ogre at all!" Pipo declared. "To sit down and eat barefoot is just not done!"

Pipo managed to convince the ogre, who proudly put on his new boots. Pipo went back to his house, happy to have saved his life, but sorry to have lost his boots.

The ogre also went home.

oberto, who envied everyone and everything, was there. Having overheard Pipo and the ogre, he had run as fast as he could to the ogre's house. He *had* to steal those boots.

Roberto trembled in his hiding-place behind the chest of drawers. Suddenly he was afraid—afraid of ending up like a tiny noodle in a big tomato sauce.

Night fell, and the ogre took off his boots to go to bed. As great snores rattled the windowpanes, Roberto slipped out of his hiding-place and put on the boots.

He escaped from the ogre's house with his new footwear. He ran like the wind until there was no wind left in him, crossing fields and forests and streams (which was not a good idea).

As soon as the boots touched the water, they grew bigger and bigger and soon became too heavy for Roberto. He was so angry at not being able to wear them that he decided to bury them, separately, in a field. If he couldn't have them, nobody else could, either.

everal days later Maria, Pipo's little sister, was planting some seeds in the field. She took her watering can and watered them.

Suddenly a giant red shape grew out of the earth.

Maria poured on more water and the shape grew larger. She yanked as hard as she could and pulled a boot out of the ground. It was her brother's boot!

Maria decided to bring the magic boot home and give it back to Pipo.

At first Pipo was delighted to get one of his boots back. But what good was it? He could not wear it: it was much too big for him. Too big for his little country, a country where people were always stepping on his feet, a country that was too small for someone whose feet kept growing.

When Maria saw how sad her brother was, she had an idea. She rolled up her little sleeves and flexed her small muscles. Then she picked up the boot and tossed it into the sea. When the boot hit the water it started growing, bigger and bigger, until it became...

...Italy!

© 1995 Rémy Simard (text)
© 1995 Pierre Pratt (art)
© 1995 English adaptation by David Homel
Design by Jeffrey Rosenberg

Annick Press Ltd

Annick Press gratefully acknowledges the support of the Canada Council and the
Ontario Arts Council.

Canadian Cataloguing in Publication Data
    Simard, Rémy
       [Bottine magique de Pipo. English]
       The magic boot

    Issued also in French under title: La bottine magique de Pipo.
    ISBN 1-55037-411-7 (bound) ISBN 1-55037-410-9 (pbk.)

    I. Pratt, Pierre. II. Title. III. Title: Bottine magique de Pipo. English.

    PS8587.I73B613 1995   jC843'.54   C95-931197-1
    PZ7.S55Ma 1995

The art in this book was rendered in acrylics.
The text was typeset in Charlotte Book.

Distributed in Canada by: Published in the U.S.A. by Annick Press (U.S.) Ltd.
Firefly Books Ltd.   Distributed in the U.S.A. by Firefly Books (U.S.) Inc.
250 Sparks Avenue   P.O. Box 1338
Willowdale, ON   Ellicott Station
M2H 2S4   Buffalo, NY 14205

Printed on acid-free paper.

Printed and bound in Canada by
Friesens, Altona, Manitoba

By the same author and illustrator:

My Dog is an Elephant
Winner, Governor General's Award
and the Mr. Christie Book Award